Cry of the Cat

Cry of the Cat

R.L. Stine

Hippo

Scholastic Children's Books
Commonwealth House, 1–19 New Oxford Street, London WC1A 1NU, UK
a division of Scholastic Ltd
London ~ New York ~ Toronto ~ Sydney ~ Auckland

First published in the USA by Scholastic Inc., 1998
First published in the UK by Scholastic Ltd, 1998

ISBN 0 590 11310 0

Typeset by Rowland Phototypesetting Ltd, Bury St Edmunds, Suffolk
Printed and bound by Mackays of Chatham

10 9 8 7

The cat opened his jaws in a shrill cry of attack. Gobs of white drool slid down his curled fangs. His yellow eyes glowed like headlights.

As he howled, the cat arched his back. His dark fur stood straight up as if shocked by electricity. The howl ended in a terrifying hiss.

The oval eyes glowed even brighter. So bright, the frightened girl had to turn away.

She pulled her brother back as the cat uttered another shrill warning cry. They stumbled back across her room until they both bumped up against the wall.

"He — he's *growing*!" she stammered, pointing with a trembling finger.

The cat's cry rose up like a wailing police siren. The creature leapt on to his hind legs. His forepaws scratched the air. Pointed claws curled out from the fur.

White drool splashed the bedroom floor as the cat hungrily flicked the points of his fangs with a purple tongue. Once again, the shrill cry ended in a long, angry hiss.

As his paws furiously raked the air, the cat grew. His hind legs stretched. His fur-shocked body appeared to inflate. The eyes — the glowing eyes — beamed above the gaping mouth.

"He's not a cat — he's a *monster!*" the girl whispered. She gripped her brother's shoulder so tight, he screamed.

"Run!" he choked out.

She turned to the bedroom door. The raging cat blocked their path. The door seemed a million miles away.

The cat opened his drooling jaws in another shrill cry. Taller than the dresser now, his shadow fell over them. He swiped a giant claw in the air. And took a heavy, lumbering step towards them.

"He wants to *eat* us!" the boy exclaimed.

The girl swallowed hard but didn't reply. She took a deep breath — and shoved her brother towards the door with both hands. "Move — *now!*"

They both hurtled to the bedroom door.

The cat's cry became a roar.

She pushed her brother again, trying to guide him around the swiping, thrashing claws.

"Nooooo!" A horrified cry escaped the girl's throat as the giant cat creature wrapped his claws round her brother's waist.

"Let go! Let go —!" She struggled to tug him free.

But the drooling cat held tight, lowered his head, and sank his long, wet fangs into the boy's shoulder.

"Stop it! Stop it! *Please* — stop it!"

My brother's terrified screams startled me. I froze for a second. Then I burst from the doorway, dived across his bedroom, and pushed the Stop button on the VCR.

The TV screen went black. I turned to the little guy. He sat on the edge of his bed, hugging himself, shaking like a terrified mouse.

"Tanner, what is your *problem*?" I scolded. "Why do you rent these frightening films? You *know* you always get scared."

"I — I'm not scared," he stammered in a tiny voice.

What a liar.

"Well . . . maybe I'm a *little* scared," he confessed, lowering his round, dark eyes to the floor.

I felt so bad for him. I wanted to hug him. But Tanner won't let anyone in the family touch him. I know it's weird. But he's just going through a stage.

"I didn't think the video would be that scary," he said, shaking his head. "The box didn't look that scary."

3

"What's the film called?" I asked.

"It's called *Cry of the Cat*."

I almost laughed. Tanner really does look like a little mouse. He's small and skinny. His black hair is cut really short, like mouse fur. And his front teeth stick out, just like mouse teeth.

"That's not a good film for a five-year-old," I scolded. "Why don't you rent cartoons or something? Why are you always terrifying yourself?" I glanced at my watch. "Uh-oh. I've got to go."

"Alison?" he asked softly, still hugging himself tightly. "Will you do me a big favour?"

"What?" I asked. "It has to be something fast, Tanner. I'm meeting Ryan. We're already late for play rehearsal."

"Could you watch the rest of the film for me?" he whimpered.

"Huh? Excuse me?" I cried.

"Could you watch it for me? I want to know what happens to the two kids."

I wanted to hug him again. He's just so cute. All of my friends are crazy about Tanner. They all want to adopt him as their little brother.

Sometimes I can't help it. Sometimes I just have to pinch his cheek or pull one of his ears. I know it breaks his No Touching rule. But he's just such a cute boy.

"Maybe later," I told him. The doorbell buzzed. "That's Ryan. I've got to go." I turned back at the door. "Are you going to be okay?"

Tanner nodded. "Wish I had a cat," he said softly.

"Huh? Why do you want a cat?" I demanded.

A sly grin spread over his face. "Because then maybe it would eat all your mice!"

I laughed. Tanner is always giving me a hard time about my mouse collection. I've got hundreds of toy mice in my room. All kinds. Stuffed mice, clay and china mice, wind-up mice. . .

"Bye," I said.

"Alison — have a *mice* day!" he called after me.

That's Tanner's big joke. He made it up himself. He's always telling me to have a *mice* day. I know it's stupid. But it's pretty good for a five-year-old.

I checked myself in my dresser mirror. I look pretty okay. I have long, straight black hair and big, round olive-green eyes. I think my nose is too long and pointy. But my mum says my face will grow into my nose.

What does that mean? I don't have a clue!

I gave my hair a quick brush and hurried outside to meet my friend Ryan Engel.

Ryan was waiting for me on his bike in the driveway. He was combing back his wavy brown hair. Ryan loves his hair. When he saw me coming, he tucked the comb in his khakis pocket and flashed me a toothy smile.

Ryan is a great-looking boy and he knows it.

But he also has a cool sense of humour, and he's smart, and he's nice.

"Ta-daaaaa!" He sang out a fanfare as I pulled my bike from the garage. "Here she is — the great Alison Moore! Take a bow!"

"Give me a break," I muttered. I swung my leg over my bike. It's a new bike. I got it for my twelfth birthday a few weeks ago. It has about a hundred zillion gears, which I haven't figured out. My old bike didn't have gears.

"Have you memorized your lines?" I asked Ryan as we started pedalling down the hill. I clicked the gears. I really didn't know what I was doing.

"Some of them," he replied. "You'll have to help me with the rest."

"Huh? How am I supposed to remember *your* part?" I cried. "I can barely keep up with mine!" I braked to slow myself as the hill sloped steeper down.

Ryan and I have the biggest parts in our school play. It's an original musical that our music teacher, Mr Keanes, wrote.

I play a royal princess in a mythical kingdom. Ryan is a thief who has entered the castle, pretending to be a prince. He steals the royal jewels, but I fall in love with him anyway.

The play is called *The Princess and the Jewel Thief*. It's very funny. But there are *soooo* many lines to learn. Plus about a dozen songs.

Ryan and I have been spending all our time trying to learn our parts. We always practise the songs as we ride our bikes the eight blocks to school.

We started singing now as we picked up speed, riding down the middle of Broad Street. The street is downhill all the way, so it's impossible to go slow.

"Wellllcome to the castle," we sang. "We know you'll have a rrrrroyal good time!"

I opened my mouth to start the next line. But I didn't get it out.

I saw the red van roaring towards us up the middle of the street.

And then I saw a blur of grey in front of my bike.

A cat?

Yes.

No time to swerve.

I tried to brake, but my hand slid off the handle.

No! The cat darted in front of me!

I felt a hard bump under the front tyre. Then I heard a harsh squeal of pain.

It all happened so fast. But I saw it all.

The cat under my bike tyre. The cat's body under the wheel.

A scrape. A *SQUISH*.

His head . . . the cat's head — came flying off the body.

7

I saw the wide-open eyes — the mouth pulled
back in surprise.

I saw the cat's head flying into the air.

And then I toppled from the bike.

I fell hard on to the road. Landed on my side.
On my arm.

The red van's horn roared in my ears.

Its tyres squealed. Too late. Too late.

Too late.

I shut my eyes.

Sharp pain shot up my body.

Then — silence. Silence all around.

I'm still breathing, I realized. I'm still here.

Cautiously, I opened my eyes. And blinked several times.

My bike had fallen on top of me.

The van stood a few metres away, the front half tilted up on the kerb. The door swung open. A young woman in a grey track suit jumped out and came running over to me.

"Alison — are you okay?" Ryan asked. He lifted the bike off my legs. The front wheel was completely mangled.

"I — I think so," I replied uncertainly. I sat up, blinking hard. I shook my head, trying to shake my dizziness away.

"I saw you fall off your bike!" the woman cried breathlessly. "Thank goodness I stopped in time." She bent over me. "Are you hurt? Can I take you somewhere? Take you home? Should we call an ambulance?"

"I think I'm okay," I groaned. I climbed unsteadily to my feet.

"What happened?" Ryan asked, still holding up my wrecked bike.

"The cat!" I cried. "I ran over the cat and —"

I shuddered, remembering the bump under my tyre. The startled expression on the cat's face as his head flew over the street.

"I *killed* him!" I wailed. "I cut off his head. The cat —"

"Do you mean *that* cat?" The woman pointed. A grey cat lay sprawled on his side, legs and body limp.

I couldn't see his head.

With a horrified gasp, I dived across the street. I knelt down beside him. The head was there. Attached to the shoulders.

The cat had a white triangle of fur behind his left ear. His yellow eyes were wide open. They stared blankly up at me.

"Is he breathing?" Ryan called.

I pressed a hand against his chest. No. No heartbeat.

My stomach lurched. I swallowed hard, trying not to puke.

Ryan was on his knees on the kerb next to me. He carefully picked up the cat. "Maybe he's okay," he murmured. "Maybe. . ."

The cat slumped limply in Ryan's arms. The eyes stared up blankly.

"He's not okay," I said in a choked whisper. "He's dead. The cat is dead. I ran over him. I killed him."

I felt the woman's hand on my shoulder. "Are you sure you're all right? I'd better get going. My son is waiting for me to pick him up."

I took the dead cat from Ryan and cradled him in my arms. Then I stood up. My leg ached from where the bike had fallen on me. And my bruised elbow throbbed. But everything else seemed okay.

I turned to the woman. "I'm fine," I told her. "Really. I'm okay."

She let out a long, relieved sigh. Ryan and I watched her climb into the van. It bumped off the kerb as she backed up.

She waved and then pulled away. I saw black skid marks in the street from where she had slammed on the brakes.

I shuddered. What a close call.

I gazed down at the dead cat. His mouth slid open. The pink tongue rolled out.

"We've got to find the owner," I murmured. "He — he ran right under my bike. I couldn't stop. You saw. It *really* wasn't my fault."

Ryan glanced at his watch. "We're *really* late for rehearsal," he said. "Mr Keanes is going to have a cow."

11

"We can't just leave a dead cat here in the street!" I told him. "We have to find his owner. I have to explain what happened."

"Is he wearing a tag?" Ryan asked.

"I can't see one."

A big, old, run-down house across the street caught my eye. "Look — the front door is open," I told Ryan, pointing. "I bet the cat ran out of that house."

We both gazed up at the house. "What a creepy-looking place!" Ryan declared. "It looks like a haunted house in a horror film!"

He was right.

The house stood half-hidden by a broken tree and tall, wild shrubs. Patches of red brick showed through the peeling grey paint. A shutter was missing from an upstairs window.

The metal guttering had fallen away from the side of the house. A side window-pane was missing, the hole stuffed with balled-up newspaper.

I wrapped the dead cat in my jacket. Then I took a deep breath and started up the driveway. Ryan held back.

"Aren't you coming with me?" I asked.

He lifted his bike off the ground by the handlebars. "I'd better get to school and tell Mr Keanes why we're late," he said.

"Chicken," I muttered.

I watched him ride off. "Hurry up!" he called

back to me. "You know Mr Keanes hates it when we're late."

I have a good excuse for being late, I thought with a sigh. I killed a living creature.

As I walked up the driveway, my jacket pulled open. The cat's grey head came into view with his triangle of white fur. The head bounced lifelessly with each step I took.

"Poor kitty," I whispered.

Halfway to the house, I heard muffled yowls and cries. Cats inside the house.

I raised my eyes to the front window — and saw several pairs of eyes staring out at me!

"So many cats!" I murmured out loud. I gazed down at the dead cat in my arms. "How many brothers and sisters did you have?"

Squinting across the garden, I could see at least a dozen dark forms perched in the front window, eyes glowing dully. The howls and yowls grew louder, sharper.

I hesitated. The cries sounded so mournful, so unhappy.

Why were they all *wailing* like that? Had they seen what I had done to their friend?

I felt a chill on the back of my neck. My heart suddenly began to pound in fear.

All those cats' eyes stared out at me so coldly from the front window. Unblinking. Unmoving.

Watching me . . . watching me so intently.

Maybe I shouldn't go up to this creepy house,

I decided. Maybe I should set the dead cat down on the front doorstep and run away from this place as fast as I can.

I shivered.

The broken tree creaked loudly behind me. The cats' sorrowful cries seemed to surround me on every side.

I stepped on to the front doorstep and peered into the open doorway. "Hello?" I called, my voice trembling and weak. I cleared my throat and tried again: "Anybody home?"

Inside the house, the cats stopped crying. I heard the shuffle of footsteps over creaking floors.

"Hello?" I called in again.

The front door swung all the way open. A girl stared out at me.

She appeared to be about my age — twelve. Maybe a year or two older.

She was very pale but quite pretty, with long brown ringlets that fell over the shoulders of her simple white smock. It hung so loosely on her, I couldn't tell if she was wearing a night-shirt or a dress.

She gazed at me with round brown eyes. Sad eyes, ringed by dark circles, as if she hadn't slept in a long time.

Behind her, the cats began to cry again.

"I — I'm sorry," I stammered. "It was an accident. I — I killed your cat."

14

I held up the bundle in my arms.

My jacket flapped open again. The dead cat stared up at us, open-mouthed.

The girl stared down at him. Her eyes bulged. She pressed her hands against her cheeks and uttered a horrified shriek: "No! No! Please — *no!*"

"I'm really sorry," I told her.

"No! Noooo!" she wailed, pressing her hands against her face, staring in horror at the limp, lifeless cat in my arms. "Not Rip! Please — not Rip!"

"He ran right under my bike tyre," I tried to explain. "I fell off my bike, and a red van was speeding. . ."

My voice trailed off. I could see that she hadn't heard a word I'd said.

"Not Rip!" she cried again. "Mum won't like this! Mum won't like this at all!"

I swallowed hard. "If you'd like me to explain to your mother —" I started.

"Rip. You killed Rip," the girl whispered, shaking her head. She raised her sad brown eyes to me, then lowered them back to the bundle in my jacket.

"Huh?" I uttered a startled cry as I felt the cat move.

He blinked his yellow eyes. Raised his head and gazed round, as if waking from a nap.

"Whoa!" My heart skipped a beat. My hands flew up. I dropped the cat.

He fell at my feet.

The cat stared up at me with his bright yellow eyes. Stared at me so coldly.

Then he scrambled away. I watched him scurry under the wild hedge. Then he vanished round the side of the house.

I gaped at him, open-mouthed, my legs trembling. "But — but he —" I couldn't speak.

Shaking all over, I turned back to the sad-eyed girl. She stared after the cat, her pale face tight with fear.

"What is your name?" she asked.

I was so upset, so shocked, it took me a few seconds to remember it. "Alison," I finally choked out.

"My name is Crystal," she said softly.

"The cat —" I cried. "He was dead. I know he was dead!"

Crystal avoided my eyes. "He's not an ordinary cat," she said through gritted teeth. "You shouldn't have messed with Rip."

"What do you mean?" I cried.

"Poor Mum," Crystal murmured.

"What do you mean?" I repeated. "What do you mean he's not an ordinary cat?"

She didn't reply. She studied me for a

moment. Then she took a step back into the house and started to close the door.

"Tell me!" I insisted. "Please. Tell me!"

"Go away!" she cried shrilly. "Just go away! I don't want that cat back! I don't ever want him back!"

And then she slammed the door.

4

I ran all the way to school and burst into the auditorium. I expected to see the rehearsal under way. But kids were sprawled around the stage, talking and laughing in groups of two and three.

Behind them, kids on the stage crew were moving big backdrops around the stage.

No sign of Mr Keanes.

"Alison — what took so long?" Ryan called down to me from the stage. He was sitting next to Freddy Weiner, who played my father, the king.

"I — I've got to talk to you," I cried breathlessly. I climbed on to the stage and frantically dragged Ryan to the curtains at the side.

"Hey — look out!" one of the kids moving a tall backdrop shouted. I nearly ran right into it.

"Alison — what is your problem?" Ryan demanded.

I shoved my hair off my face with both hands. "The cat —" I choked out. "He came to life!"

Ryan stared at me as if I were speaking some strange language.

"He was dead, Ryan," I continued excitedly. "You saw him — right? I carried him up to the old house. A girl recognized him. She acted really weird. She called him Rip. She started screaming and . . . and. . ."

I said all that without taking a breath.

Ryan continued to stare at me.

"And then the cat came back to life!" I cried. "He opened his eyes, gave me an angry look — and ran away."

Ryan laughed.

"What's so funny?" I demanded.

"He gave you an angry look?" he asked.

"Yes," I insisted. "It was so strange, Ryan. The girl was so weird. And . . . and. . ."

"So the story has a happy ending," he interrupted. "The cat wasn't dead, after all."

"But he *was* dead!" I cried. "You saw him —"

"Maybe he was only dazed," Ryan said.

Some of the scenery people dropped a heavy backdrop, and everyone clapped and cheered.

"The cat must have been in shock or something," Ryan said. "Then he woke up, and he was okay."

I thought about it. "I suppose you're right," I

told him. "There is no other way to explain it. But . . . the girl really frightened me. She said Rip wasn't an ordinary cat. She said I shouldn't have messed with Rip."

Ryan sniggered. "She was probably trying to scare you."

"But she seemed really frightened herself," I replied.

Ryan shrugged.

"Where is Mr Keanes?" I asked, glancing round the auditorium.

"Late," Ryan replied. "Lucky, huh? We won't get a lecture."

"Yeah. Lucky," I agreed. But I couldn't stop thinking about Crystal and Rip.

I was still thinking about them when Mr Keanes finally came bursting on to the stage, clapping his chubby hands. "People! People! Can we begin our scene now?"

I grabbed my cardboard crown off the throne and slid it over my hair. Ryan stepped into place, using a walking-stick as a cane.

"So sorry I'm late," Mr Keanes said, hurrying across the stage, clipboard pressed over the front of his brown cardigan.

With his big, round glasses, his round, balding head, and his egg-shaped body, Mr Keanes looks like a chubby owl.

He acts a little birdlike too. He's always ruffling his arms, pulling at his sweater, tilting his head from one side to the other as he watches us.

He gets impatient with us sometimes. But he's a really good teacher, and he's really talented. He wrote all the songs for our play in less than a week!

"Where shall we begin?" He peered down at his clipboard. "Oh, yes. The king is introducing Sir Frances to you, Princess."

He raised his eyes to me and squinted at the purple bruise on my elbow. "What did you do to yourself, Alison?"

"Fell off my bike," I told him.

Once again, I pictured the blur of grey fur and felt the bump under my tyre. And saw the cat's head with his yellow eyes flying over the street.

Mr Keanes tsk-tsked. "Did you wash it? Did you put anything on it?"

"I'll do it right after rehearsal," I replied. "I was late. So. . ."

"I don't think Princess Aurora would walk around the palace like that," he scolded. He took a breath. "Okay. Places." He waved to Freddy Weiner. "You begin, King Raymond."

Freddy started to talk, but his voice cracked. Kids on the scenery crew and others hanging out in the auditorium laughed and clapped.

Freddy cleared his throat and started again. "Princess Aurora, my daughter, we have a royal visitor from afar."

"Oh, really, Father?" I replied, standing straight and tall as a royal person.

"Allow me to introduce the prince," Freddy said, sweeping his hand towards Ryan.

Ryan leaned on his walking-stick and took a deep bow. He started to talk. But I didn't hear his words.

I heard a cry from across the stage.

A loud *MEOW*.

I turned to the sound, lowering my gaze to the floor.

"*MEEEEOW.*"

I pushed past Freddy and dropped down to my knees on the stage, searching for the cat.

"Alison — is anything wrong?" Mr Keanes demanded. He stood on the auditorium floor. His round head barely poked up over the stage floor.

"That cat . . ." I murmured.

He cried out again. A little softer. Sort of a mewing sound.

"Where is he?" I cried. "Can anybody see him?"

A couple of kids on the stage crew stared at me from backstage. "Can you *hear* him?" I called to them.

They shook their heads.

"Alison — I can't see a cat," Mr Keanes called impatiently. "Could we continue the scene?"

24

"I *heard* him!" I insisted. "Clear as day."

I saw Freddy roll his eyes. Ryan hurried over to me. "Are you sure you're okay?"

"Yeah. Fine," I replied. "I heard a cat. That's all."

Ryan studied me for a long moment. "You had a really bad fall. Maybe —"

"I didn't fall on my head!" I cried. "I'm not *crazy*, Ryan! I heard a cat!"

I suppose I was shouting. I turned and saw everyone in the auditorium staring at me.

"Places — please, people!" Mr Keanes pleaded.

I followed Ryan back to the centre of the stage. And heard the cat's cry again, from very near by.

"Did you hear that?" I cried. Ryan and Freddy stared at me blankly.

"Alison, please continue," Mr Keanes urged from the auditorium floor. "Walk to the chamber cabinet now," he instructed. "Remove the royal sceptre and bring it to King Raymond."

"Okay," I said. I started towards the wooden cabinet across the stage.

"King Raymond, what is your line?" Mr Keanes demanded.

Freddy's mouth dropped open. I could see he was having trouble remembering. We hadn't rehearsed this part of the scene yet.

"Uh . . . Princess Aurora, please bring out the royal sceptre." He finally remembered.

I stepped up to the cabinet. Pulled open the door.

Two yellow eyes stared out at me.

I heard a shrill, angry cry.

And saw two raised paws.

Before I could move, the cat flew from the top shelf.

He landed on my face.

I cried out as the claws dug into my shoulders.

With a furious hiss, the cat raised his head. His yellow eyes flared like the sun.

"No! Help!"

I let out a shriek — and stumbled backwards as the cat bared his curved fangs and lowered them to my throat.

6

"Ohhhh — help!"

I grabbed for the cat with both hands.

He let out an ugly shriek as I pulled him off my face — and *flung* him away from me with all my strength.

My heart pounding, I watched him sail across the stage. His yellow eyes bulged. His mouth was pulled open in another deafening screech.

It all happened so fast.

Two boys were hoisting the heavy throne off the stage. One of them cried out as the cat flew towards him.

The cat hit the boy's shoulder. He bounced to the floor.

The startled boys dropped the throne.

I heard a sickening *CRACK* as the throne landed on top of the cat.

Silence.

For a few seconds, no one moved.

Then, as I stood frozen in place, my hands over my eyes, everyone moved and cried out at once.

"Is he crushed?"

"Is he dead?"

"What *was* that?"

"Whose cat was that?"

"How did he get in the cabinet?"

I heard Mr Keanes ordering the boys to lift the throne. Then I heard groans of disgust.

"Ohhhh, yuck!"

"You *flattened* him."

A boy laughed. "Roadkill!"

Two girls shouted at him to shut up.

"I'm going to be sick," a girl groaned. She went running off-stage.

I swallowed hard and followed Ryan over to the cat. My legs trembled. I tasted blood on my bottom lip. I hadn't realized I'd been biting it.

Freddy was bending over the cat, shaking his head. "Oh, wow," Ryan murmured, dropping down beside Freddy.

I squatted beside him. Holding my breath, I stared down at the cat. "Oh, no!" I cried. "Ryan —"

"He's dead," he murmured.

"Ryan — it's the same cat!" I cried. "I killed him! I killed him *again*!"

"Alison, are you okay? Did he bite you?" Mr

28

Keanes came bouncing across the stage, his face bright red.

"No, I'm okay," I replied shakily.

I turned back to Ryan. "Look at him! The grey fur. The white triangle behind his ear. The same cat!"

"The same cat as *what*?" Freddy demanded.

Ryan studied the cat. "No way, Alison," he replied. "He can't be." He picked him up between his hands. He slumped lifelessly, limp as a rag.

Freddy groaned in disgust. "Yuck."

"But he *is*!" I insisted. "He's the same cat. I know he is! I ran over this cat. And now he's — he's back!"

"Will somebody please tell me what is going on here?" Mr Keanes demanded.

As I turned to answer him, the cat suddenly kicked out all four legs.

Freddy, Ryan and I all screamed.

Ryan let him fall from his hands.

The cat landed on his feet with a *THUD*. He scurried over my trainers — and ran to the edge of the stage.

"Stop him!" Freddy yelled. "Catch him!"

But before anyone could move, the cat leapt off the stage and disappeared under the auditorium seats.

I saw a few kids go after him. But they quickly gave up. The cat had vanished.

"He was the *same cat*!" I told Ryan. "It happened again! He was dead — and — and — he came back to life!"

"Take it easy, Alison," Ryan replied, staring hard at me.

I could see he didn't believe me. But I knew I was right.

I had accidentally killed the cat twice. And both times he had sprung back to life and run away.

"He *attacked* me!" I declared with a shudder. "He jumped out of the cabinet and *attacked* me."

Ryan shook his head. "The cat was frightened. That's all. He got locked in the cabinet. When you opened the door, he jumped out. He didn't know you were standing there."

"But — but how did he get in there?" I stammered.

Ryan twisted up his face, thinking hard.

But before he could reply, Mr Keanes interrupted. "People! People!" he cried, motioning with both hands for us to gather round him. "I can see that you're all very upset about that cat. What a strange thing! I'm going to end rehearsal for today. See you all tomorrow. The time is on the rehearsal schedule."

Mr Keanes came over to me. "You sure you're okay, Alison? I could get you a lift home."

"No, thanks. I'll be fine," I told him. "It — it's just been a strange day."

Ryan, Freddy and I started walking off-stage.

"*MEEE-OW!*"

I gasped when I heard the shrill cat cry.

"Where is he?" I cried. "Where is he *now*?"

7

"MEEOW."

I heard him again.

Then I saw Freddy's grin and I realized he was doing the meowing.

"*MEEEEOW*." He clawed at me with one hand.

"Freddy," I asked, "did anyone ever tell you you're not funny?"

"Everyone," he replied, still grinning.

At dinner that night, I told Mum, Dad and Tanner about running over the cat. "He ran right under my bike," I explained. "At first, I thought I saw his head fly off. But no. I suppose I imagined that. I felt a bump under the tyre and —"

"Yuck." Tanner made a face. "Did you really *squish* him?"

"This isn't very good dinner-table conversation," Dad interrupted. "Could we talk about something else?"

"Did you kill him?" Tanner demanded, leaning over his soup bowl.

Mum set a soup bowl down in front of me. "Your father is right, Alison. Don't upset your brother. Change the subject."

"Delicious soup, Margo," Dad told Mum.

I lowered my spoon into the soup, but I didn't taste it. "I wrecked my bike," I told Dad.

Mum sneezed.

Dad narrowed his eyes at me. "Your new bike?"

I nodded. My stomach tightened with dread. I knew he'd be angry.

"How *could* you wreck it?" he screamed. "It's a brand-new bike!"

"Please —" Mum raised a hand in a halt sign — "let's talk about it after dinner. I made this chicken noodle soup from scratch. Could we just relax and enjoy it?"

She sneezed again. She wiped her nose with her napkin.

"Weird," she muttered. "I feel strange."

Dad swallowed a mouthful of soup and squinted across the table at Mum. "Your face, Margo — you look a little puffy."

"I feel the way I do when there's a cat near by," Mum said. "My allergy —" She sneezed again.

"Maybe because Alison was talking about a cat," Tanner suggested.

Wiping her nose, Mum laughed. "I'm not allergic to *talking* about a cat!" Her eyes were running.

Dad turned to me, frowning. "Alison, that cat you ran over on your bike. Did you bring him home with you?"

"No!" I cried. "I didn't bring any cat home!"

Mum sniffed and dabbed the napkin at her runny eyes. "Maybe you have cat fur on your clothes," she said to me.

I pushed back my chair and started to stand up. "Should I run upstairs and change?"

"No, Alison. Sit down," Mum ordered. She glanced round the table. "I made this delicious home-made chicken noodle soup, and no one is eating it."

"I am!" Dad declared. He slurped a long noodle between his lips. "It's excellent."

"Mine is too hot," Tanner whined.

"It is not," Mum scolded. "Eat your soup. Both of you."

Watching Tanner blow on his soup bowl, I raised the spoon and took a big mouthful.

It tasted a little strange.

I chewed.

And chewed.

Something wrong. I couldn't swallow it. Something prickly stuck to my tongue.

"Aaaaaaah." I uttered a disgusted groan. Stuck out my tongue. And pulled clumps of stuff from my mouth with two fingers.

"What *is* this?" I cried.

Grey shreds. Like whiskers.

No. Like fur.

Grey cat fur!

"Nooooo!" I let out a sick moan and stared down into my soup . . . into the bowl . . . the bowl . . . steaming and dark . . . bubbling with cat fur.

"Aaaaack! I can't get it out of my mouth!" I shrieked.

I gagged and started to choke.

Dad jumped up and started slamming me on the back.

I coughed up a wet chunk of cat fur. Then I jammed my napkin into my mouth and frantically tried to mop the fur off my tongue.

"I don't understand it," Mum murmured. She held my soup bowl close to her face and shook her head. "I just don't understand it. How did that stuff get in there?"

I gagged again. I spun away from the table and ran to the mirror in the front hall. I pulled back my lips and leant close to the mirror.

"Ohhhh," I moaned. "I've got fur stuck between my teeth!"

I heard Tanner start to cry. "Take it away! Take the soup away!" he wailed.

"But it was perfectly good soup!" I heard Mum declare.

Holding my hand over my mouth, I ran up to my bathroom. I brushed my teeth for at least half an hour. There was grey cat hair all over the sink.

My mouth still felt gritty. My tongue still itched.

"What is happening?" I cried out to my unhappy face in the mirror. "What is going on round here?"

Still feeling shaky, I made my way down the hall to my room. I stopped outside the door. The *closed* door.

That's weird, I thought. I know I left this door open.

Why is it closed now? Who closed it?

Alison, you're starting to go over the edge, I scolded myself.

Who *cares* if your bedroom door is closed? What is the big deal?

I gripped the doorknob, turned it, pushed open the door — and screamed, "Nooooooo! Oh *no*!"

Gripping the doorknob, I stared into the room in disbelief.

The room was a *disaster*!

"My mice —!" I cried out loud.

The glass display cases were empty. My whole collection of toy mice was scattered all over the room.

Mice had been thrown over the floor, on to my bedspread, over my desktop — *everywhere*!

The waste-paper basket overflowed with mice. They'd been stuck into the folds of my window curtains. A white stuffed mouse poked its head out of the ceiling light.

"Who?" I cried. "Who did this?"

I stood in the doorway, hands pressed against my cheeks, and gazed round the room. I own at least two hundred little mice. Someone had taken them all down, had thrown them everywhere.

Blinking, I pictured the grey cat again.

Rip. Rip . . .

Crystal's words repeated chillingly in my ears. *"That's not an ordinary cat . . . You shouldn't have messed with Rip."*

I had killed him. Killed him twice.

And now he was out to get me. He was in my room, my own bedroom!

I sighed. That cat couldn't have anything to do with this, I told myself. How could he get into the house? How could he know where I live?

Alison, don't start thinking crazy thoughts. There wasn't any cat in your room, throwing your mice around. You've spent too much time watching Tom & Jerry cartoons on TV with Tanner.

Tanner.

I turned and saw him standing in the doorway. His eyes were wide. His chin trembled, the way it always does when he is tense or upset. He looked so tiny and cute in his Godzilla T-shirt and baggy khakis.

"Alison — what happened?" he cried.

I tried to make a joke. "Earthquake," I said. "Can you believe it? An eight-point-six earthquake, and it hit only in my bedroom!"

He didn't smile. He walked into the room, stepping carefully over a couple of plastic wind-up mice.

"Did the display shelf fall?" he asked.

39

I motioned to it with my head. "Still there," I muttered.

"Did *you* take them all out?" he asked.

"Uh . . . yeah," I lied. I didn't want to frighten him any more than I had. I forced myself to keep my voice steady and calm. "I took them down this morning," I said.

He narrowed his dark eyes at me. "Why?"

"Uh . . . I want to reorganize them," I said, thinking quickly. "Put all the stuffed ones together, all the wind-ups in another pile. You know."

He nodded. But I could see he was thinking hard about what I was telling him.

I shivered. "Maybe after dinner you can help me put all the mice back in the right places."

"Okay," he agreed, still staring hard at me. "Unless I'm busy watching TV or something."

I waited until he went downstairs. Then I started to clean up.

I didn't have the patience to put all the mice back in the display cases. I gathered them up as fast as I could, throwing them into a big laundry bag. I shoved the laundry bag into my wardrobe.

Then I made my way back downstairs.

In school the next day, I hurried over to Ryan's table in the canteen. I dropped my brown-paper lunch bag next to his and sank into the chair across from him.

"You look terrible," he said.

"Gee, thanks," I muttered, rolling my eyes. I pushed my hair back off my forehead.

"No. I mean, you look tired," he explained. "You have dark circles under your eyes."

"I didn't sleep much," I confessed. "Every time I closed my eyes, I saw that cat."

He squinted at me. "The grey cat? Did you see him again?"

"No," I told him. "But I think he was in my house."

"You're kidding — right?" He reached for his lunch bag.

I grabbed his arm to stop him. "Don't eat yet," I said. "First I want to tell you what happened last night at dinner."

I told him about the wet clump of fur I'd swallowed. About the disgusting cat fur in my chicken noodle soup.

He stuck his finger down his throat and made gagging sounds. "I may never eat again!" he declared.

"It isn't funny, Ryan," I insisted. "I could have choked to death on that fur."

"But that's crazy. How did it get in the soup?" he demanded.

I shrugged. "I think it was Rip. I don't know how. I can't explain it."

"Yuck." Ryan looked genuinely sick.

I told him about my toy mouse collection scattered all over the room. "I think that cat was in there," I said. "I know it sounds stupid. But you saw that cat. He was dead, right? He was crushed. And he came back to life. Maybe he has powers, Ryan. Maybe . . ."

Ryan scrunched up his face the way he always does when he is thinking hard. He squinted at me across the table. "Your toy mice were thrown everywhere? Are you sure your little brother isn't having a little fun with you?"

"Huh?" My mouth dropped open. "Tanner?"

Ryan nodded.

"No way," I insisted. "Tanner has never played a trick on anyone in his life. It just isn't like him. You know how scared he gets about things."

"You've got to stop thinking about that cat," Ryan warned. "I know you feel bad . . ."

"I killed him twice!" I cried. Several kids turned to stare at me. I lowered my voice and leant across the table. "I killed him twice, and he came back to life. And now, he's out to get me."

Ryan studied me for a long time. "You know how crazy that sounds," he said finally.

I nodded. "What is *your* explanation?" I demanded.

I knew he didn't have an explanation. "Let's

eat," he mumbled, eyeing the big clock over the canteen door. "It's getting late. No more cat talk."

I grabbed the brown-paper lunch bag. "Okay, okay," I said.

I pulled open the bag, peered inside — and gasped.

"Alison — what's wrong?" Ryan cried.

I stared into the bag. "This isn't my lunch," I replied.

"Huh?" He squinted across the table at me.

"It's *your* lunch," I said. "I took the wrong bag by mistake."

He let out a long sigh. "What is your problem? You scared me to death." He grabbed his lunch bag and shoved mine across the table to me.

"I'm sorry," I murmured. "I didn't mean to gasp like that. I'm just a little freaked out. You know."

"Well, try to unfreak yourself," Ryan growled. He pulled out a sandwich wrapped in aluminium foil. "What have you got for lunch? Want to swap? I think this is egg salad. Egg salad always reminds me of dog vomit."

"Thanks for sharing that," I replied, rolling my eyes.

"Well? What have you got?" he demanded.

44

I pulled open the bag and gazed inside.

Two bright yellow eyes stared up at me.

Two eyes surrounded by grey fur. I stared at whiskers that scraped the sides of the bag. An open mouth, revealing curved teeth. A purple tongue rolling stiffly out.

With a horrified cry, I leapt to my feet. The chair clattered to the floor behind me.

"Noooooooo!" I wailed.

I saw kids turning in shock to stare. But I couldn't stop myself. I couldn't stop myself from screaming.

"The cat! The cat's head! The head! In the bag! Ohhhh, help! Please — somebody, help! His head is in the bag!"

"Wonderful, people! That was wonderful!" Mr Keanes cried. His voice echoed through the nearly empty auditorium. "You made me believe it that time!"

Ryan, Freddy and I took a bow.

It was our first night rehearsal, and it had gone really well. We were finally remembering our lines and we were able to move more comfortably around the stage.

Having such a good rehearsal helped me forget — at least for a short while — about lunch.

I never wanted to think about it again. I wished I could wipe the memory from my mind for ever.

It was all so embarrassing. So completely humiliating.

Ryan grabbed the lunch bag. Tore it open. No cat head inside. Just a sandwich and a green apple.

He held the apple up. "Alison, is *this* what you saw?" he demanded. "Is *this* it?"

I stood gripping the table with both hands, my whole body trembling.

I could see everyone in the canteen staring at me.

"I ... didn't ... imagine it," I managed to choke out to Ryan through gritted teeth. Then I spun away and ran out of the canteen.

I ran as fast as I could. Ran to my locker. Grabbed my jacket and books and ran home.

I didn't stop running until I was inside the house. I pulled myself up the stairs to my room, slammed the door shut, and threw myself face down on to the bed.

"I'm never coming out!" I cried out loud. "Never! Never! Never!"

Ryan called after school to see if I was okay. And to remind me about the night rehearsal.

I worried about going back to school. I thought the kids might laugh at me and make cat sounds when they saw me. But everyone acted as if the scene in the canteen had never happened. Even Freddy.

Then, we had a really good rehearsal. That cheered me up a lot.

Mr Keanes perched on the piano bench at the side of the stage and looked on, beaming proudly. A spotlight made his bald head glow.

"Scene two, people!" he announced, clapping

47

his pudgy hands. "Places. Scene two. Come on. Places, everyone. Make it as snappy as scene one."

As I walked to my place in the throne room, I felt my good mood fade away. My stomach knotted and my throat tightened. This was the scene I'd been dreading.

I glanced at the cabinet at the side of the stage. And remembered the shrieking cat leaping out at me when I pulled open the doors.

I stared hard at the cabinet doors, as if trying to see through the wood.

Is Rip in there, waiting to pounce? I wondered. Am I going to be attacked again?

"Alison — are you okay?" Ryan asked.

I forced myself to turn away from the cabinet. "Uh . . . yeah. I suppose so," I replied uncertainly.

My problem is that I can't stop thinking about that horrible cat! I thought unhappily.

I shut my eyes, trying to clear my mind.

"Okay. Let's begin," Mr Keanes called.

"Princess Aurora, please bring out the royal sceptre," Freddy, the king, ordered.

I gazed at him blankly, my heart pounding.

"The royal sceptre," he repeated, motioning to the cabinet.

I saw everyone staring at me. Waiting.

"Oh. Right," I uttered.

I walked over to the cabinet. I raised my hands to the two wooden doorknobs.

I hesitated, listening for the sound of a cat inside the cabinet.

Silence.

I swallowed hard. My mouth was suddenly as dry as cotton.

I didn't want to pull open those doors. I really didn't want to.

But I had no choice.

I took a deep breath — and jerked both cabinet doors open at once.

"Oh!" A sharp cry escaped my lips.

Nothing inside.

No cat. No living creature.

I picked up the silvery sceptre, spun away from the cabinet, and crossed the stage to present it to the king.

I knew I had a big smile on my face, which didn't belong in the scene. I couldn't help it. I felt so relieved.

Maybe that cat has finished with me, I thought. Maybe he has stopped chasing me.

I was wrong.

I didn't get home till nearly eleven, but I didn't feel sleepy. I think I was too pumped up from the rehearsal. So excited it had gone so well.

Mr Keanes had given out lyric sheets for some of the songs in the play. I took them up to my room and read them over for a while, trying to memorize the words.

I thought about calling Ryan and going over the songs with him. But it was too late.

So I practised by myself.

After a while, I started to yawn. My eyelids began to feel heavy.

Time for bed.

I dropped the lyric sheets on my desk and crossed to my dresser to get a nightshirt.

"Oh!" I cried out when I saw the creature on the floor.

A mouse!

No. It didn't move.

Bending down, I saw that it was a grey plastic wind-up mouse. I must have missed it when I'd cleaned up.

"So real looking," I muttered. Yawning, I tucked it into my jeans pocket.

I changed, turned off the light, dropped wearily into bed. Before I realized it, I drifted into a deep, dreamless sleep.

I didn't sleep long.

I woke up choking.

I couldn't breathe!

I stared into total blackness.

Something heavy and warm covered my face.

Sharp nails dug into the shoulders of my nightshirt.

My hands shot up and grabbed wildly.

I felt fur. Warm skin underneath.

A cat!

A cat wrapped over my face. Pressed so tight. Holding on . . . holding on . . .

Covering me in heavy darkness.

Choking me . . .

Suffocating me.

Pools of blackness swirled over my face. The black slowly brightened to bright red.

My chest ached. My lungs felt about to burst.

With a last, desperate sweep of my arms, I grasped the cat's furry back with both hands — and tugged it up a few centimetres.

My chest heaving, I sucked in a mouthful of air.

The cat kicked and thrashed. But I kept my grasp on his back. And lifted him higher.

My temples pulsed. I sucked in another breath of air. I let it out in a whoosh and sucked in another. The sweetest breaths I'd ever taken.

I started to feel a little stronger. Groaning, I pulled myself up, still gripping the cat in both hands. His four legs kicked furiously. His claws swiped viciously at my face.

And he grabbed me again!

"No!" I shrieked.

I raised the cat high — and with a desperate groan, heaved him across the room.

Heaved him high. Harder than I'd planned.

I stared in shock as the cat sailed across the room — and hurtled out of the open window.

I heard him cry out. Then I heard a hard *THUD* as he hit the ground below.

Then silence.

"Oh, no," I murmured in a choked whisper.

I forced myself out of bed and dived to the window on trembling legs. Leaning over the sill, I peered down at the back garden.

In the light of the full moon, I saw the cat sprawled on his back, his head twisted to one side, his four paws straight up in the air.

Even from my bedroom window high above the ground, I recognized the cat.

Rip.

And I knew without going down there that I had killed him again. Killed him for a *third* time.

But will he stay dead? The frightening question repeated in my mind. *Will he stay dead this time?*

I crept to my wardrobe and pulled a long raincoat over my nightshirt. Then I made my way out to the garden to make sure.

The grass felt icy and wet on the soles of my bare feet. The moonlight made the garden glow like silver.

My heart pounded as I leant down to examine the cat.

Yes. The same cat. Rip. Rip once again.

Not breathing. Not moving.

His yellow eyes locked in a glassy, blank stare. His legs stiff and straight, pointing up to the moon.

Rip. Dead for the third time. Rip. The cat that refused to stay dead.

I wanted to shout for my parents. Wanted to shout at the top of my lungs. *"Come and see this dead cat — before he runs away again!"*

But they would never believe me.

The cat would vanish before they saw him. Vanish the way the cat's head had disappeared from the lunch bag.

I leant over the dead cat and screamed at him. "Why are you doing this to me? Why are you *haunting* me?"

I saw the cat's eyes blink. I saw the head straighten up. I saw the paws snap back.

But I couldn't move. Couldn't get away in time.

And Rip swiped a claw at me. Dug his long claws into my skin. And slashed a long, deep wound down my leg.

I cried out as burning pain roared up my leg, up my side. I grabbed my leg, gasping, trying to squeeze away the pain.

The cat jumped to his feet. He arched his back. Pulled back his lips in a menacing hiss. Prepared to attack again.

"No!" I uttered a sharp cry of protest. Holding my leg, I spun round and frantically hobbled across the wet grass towards the house.

The pain didn't fade. It soared up from my wounded leg. My head throbbed. I felt so dizzy, I had to grab the kitchen door-frame to stop myself from falling over.

In the house, I turned and squinted back across the silvery lawn. The cat hadn't moved. He stood glaring at me with those evil yellow eyes.

Hissing, he scraped a paw in the air again and again, as if clawing me, as if warning me about what he wanted to do to me.

With a shudder, I slammed the back door.

Then, holding my leg, I pulled myself up the stairs to the bathroom. The pain had finally faded, but my head still spun. My whole body seemed to pulse and throb.

I clicked on the light. Staggered to the sink. Grabbed up a handful of tissues to press against the scratch to stop the bleeding.

I bent over. Lowered the tissues to the wound — and gasped in surprise.

It wasn't bleeding.

The deep scratch marks were a bright white, so bright they appeared to glow.

The scratches cut through the skin — but no blood seeped out. No blood at all.

I stared at my leg, rubbing my hand over it gently, soothing away the lingering pain.

Cuts are supposed to bleed — aren't they? I asked myself. Cuts are always red. Never bright white.

And they always bleed — *don't they?*

The next morning, my clock radio woke me at seven-thirty. I sat up and stretched. Then I stuck out my injured leg to examine it.

Blinking away sleep, I squinted hard at it. Rubbed my fingers over it. Studied the leg again.

To my amazement, the deep white scratch marks had completely vanished.

I climbed to my feet, feeling shaky and still tired. I'm a morning person. I usually wake up feeling cheerful and ready to go. But this morning, I felt so tired, as if I hadn't slept at all. And as I dragged myself across the room to get dressed for school, my body seemed to weigh a thousand pounds!

"Mum?" I called, stepping into the kitchen a short while later. She was standing in the middle of the room, twisting her hands behind her, struggling to fasten buttons on the back of her blouse.

"Mum — I have to tell you something," I blurted out. "About last night." I stepped up behind her and did the buttons for her.

"A man had to design this blouse," she said, frowning. "Only a man would make a blouse that you can't button yourself. Do you think a man would ever buy a shirt that had the buttons down the back? Of course not."

"Mum, please —" I started.

She slammed a box of cornflakes on the breakfast table. Then hurried to the fridge and pulled out a carton of milk. "Make yourself some cereal, Alison. Get some juice from the fridge. I'm in a terrible hurry. I'm already late."

"But I have to tell you something!" I protested.

She didn't hear me. She hurried out to the hall to get something.

When she's in a big rush, she doesn't hear a word anyone says. And Mum is *usually* in a rush.

I went to the cabinet and searched the bottom shelf. "Where's Tanner?" I called.

"Left early. With your father," Mum called back. "Where is my purse? Why can't I ever find my purse?"

I pulled some things from the cabinet. The kitchen radio was on on the other side of the room. A news report. Something about a hurricane.

I started to eat.

Mum stepped back into the kitchen, biting her bottom lip fretfully. "I'm retracing my steps," she said. "That purse has to be somewhere."

"I really have to talk to you," I tried again. "There's a big grey cat —"

Mum disappeared again.

"Found it!" she called from somewhere in the back.

I stood at the worktop, eating my breakfast. Sunlight poured in from the kitchen window, sending splashes of yellow around the room. The back door was open. I heard children laughing and shouting somewhere down the block.

Despite the cheerful day, I still felt tired and gloomy. I couldn't stop thinking about Rip.

"*He's not an ordinary cat.*" Crystal's frightened words came back to me. *"You shouldn't have messed with Rip."*

I swallowed down my breakfast hungrily. Standing at the worktop, I shuddered when I thought of the cat covering my face as I slept.

What was he trying to do?

Was he really trying to smother me?

I pictured him sailing out of the window. I remembered the hard *THUD* as he landed on the ground two storeys below.

He died. But he didn't die.

"Mum — I've really got to talk to you!" I shouted.

"Alison, you don't have to shout." She startled me. She was standing a few metres away, in the kitchen doorway.

"Mum —" I started.

But her eyes were on the worktop. Her face filled with alarm. "Alison — what on earth are you doing?" she cried. "What kind of breakfast is *that*?"

I looked down — and let out a startled cry. "Oh, no. I don't believe it!"

I stared in horror at the empty cans on the kitchen worktop.

I had gobbled down three cans of tuna, right from the can.

At play rehearsal that afternoon, I felt a little better. I didn't have my usual energy. But at least I didn't feel so shaky and weird.

I just need a good night's sleep, I decided. I need a night without a mysterious cat climbing over my face. I made my way down the rows of auditorium seats and climbed on to the stage.

Ryan and Freddy were arm-wrestling beside the royal throne in the centre of the stage. Freddy was so much bigger than Ryan, he barely had to strain. Ryan's face was bright red and twisted in pain as Freddy pushed his arm down.

Other kids urged them on, cheering and laughing.

At stage right, kids on the crew were working on the castle balcony. It was actually a tall cardboard cut-out, strapped on to the front of a very tall ladder.

In the last act, I had to climb the ladder and

lean over the balcony as I talked with Ryan. I'd already tested the ladder a few times. It was a bit shaky.

I don't like heights to begin with. Climbing up there made me really nervous. But Mr Keanes had promised that the ladder would be solidly anchored.

"Just watch your step as you climb it," he'd told me, "and you'll be perfectly fine."

I dropped my rucksack at the side of the stage. Then I walked over to the throne.

As I approached, Freddy slammed Ryan's hand down hard on the throne arm. Freddy jumped up, raising both hands over his head in triumph as the other kids cheered.

Still red-faced, Ryan moved away, scowling and shaking his hand in pain.

"Never try to arm-wrestle with the *king*!" Freddy called after him.

I hurried over to Ryan. "I think Freddy is starting to take his part in the play too seriously," I said. "Since when does he call himself *king*?"

Ryan shook his hand some more. "He cheated," he muttered. "I almost had him, but he cheated."

I couldn't help myself. I laughed. "How do you cheat at arm-wrestling?" I demanded.

"By being bigger and stronger than me!" Ryan exclaimed.

We both laughed.

"Where is Mr Keanes?" I asked.

"He's in the office, talking to a parent," Freddy said, tossing his king's crown from hand to hand. He motioned to the ladder. "Alison, are you ready for the balcony scene?"

I gazed at the tall ladder. The kids on the stage crew were having trouble attaching the cardboard balcony cut-out. One of them let out a cry as the whole thing nearly toppled over.

"Maybe we won't do it today," I said. "I haven't had time to learn my lines for that scene."

Freddy turned to Ryan. "How's your hand? I didn't break it, did I?" He grinned.

"It's okay," Ryan replied, scowling. "Next time, I'll give you a few pointers."

"Next time?" Freddy laughed. "You're ready to go again?"

Ryan avoided Freddy's gaze. "Maybe tomorrow," he muttered.

We kidded around for a while, waiting for Mr Keanes. Down at the seats, some kids in the chorus started to rehearse one of the songs.

The stage crew finally got the balcony hooked on to the ladder. They all climbed down to admire it.

Ryan was talking about a funny thing that had happened in Mr Clay's art class earlier in the afternoon. Ryan does a perfect imitation of Mr Clay's high, shrill voice.

We were all laughing and trying to sound like Mr Clay too.

Suddenly, Ryan stopped. His smile faded. He narrowed his eyes at me. "Alison — what is your problem?" he asked. "Why are you doing that?"

"Weird!" Freddy cried. "Why are you licking the back of your hands?"

I gave the back of my left hand a few more licks. Then I examined both hands. Perfectly clean now.

I dried them on the legs of my jeans.

"Hey —" I demanded. "Why is everyone staring at me?"

A short while later, Mr Keanes finally arrived, and we started to rehearse.

Mr Keanes seemed more frantic than usual. He kept bouncing round the stage, interrupting us every few seconds, scribbling furiously on his clipboard. After only a few minutes, he had big sweat stains under the arms of his shirt.

I suppose he's nervous because the play performance is only a week away, I thought. I felt a little nervous too. How would I ever memorize all my lines by then?

I jumped and spun round when I thought I heard a cat's cry. But it was only the squeak of a folding chair being opened in the auditorium.

When I turned back, Mr Keanes was staring at me. "Didn't you hear me, Alison?" he asked, peering at me over those round glasses of his. "I said let's try the balcony scene."

"Oh. Sorry." I turned and made my way quickly to the ladder at the side of the stage.

Mr Keanes asked two boys to hold it steady for me.

"Here goes," I murmured. I took a deep breath and started to climb.

"How is it?" Mr Keanes called. "Pretty steady?"

"Yeah. Not bad," I replied. I gripped the sides of the ladder tightly and pulled myself up rung by rung.

Alison, don't look down, I instructed myself.

But, of course, I couldn't help it. I glanced down at Ryan, Freddy and the others in the cast. They were all watching me climb.

I was breathing hard by the time I reached the top. I gripped the edge of the cardboard balcony and peered out.

"How's the weather up there?" Freddy called.

"Not bad!" I shouted down. "It's a little cloudy, but —"

"It's getting late. Let's try the scene," Mr Keanes interrupted impatiently. "Ryan, take your place."

Ryan scratched his head. "Where do I go?"

Mr Keanes motioned with the clipboard. "Under the balcony. Yes. That's right. Now, remember, Alison, you're very angry with him. You've just discovered that he's not a prince. He's a fake. And you want to pay him back for tricking you."

"I've got it," I called down from my high perch. "Anger. I'll be angry, Mr Keanes."

He nodded and motioned for Ryan to start.

But before Ryan could open his mouth, Jenny, one of the secretaries in the head-teacher's office, came running down the centre aisle of the auditorium. "Alison! Alison!" she called.

I stared down at her.

"Alison? Phone call for you," she called up to me. "It's your mum."

"Huh? Is everything okay?" I cried.

"Yes. But she said she needs to talk to you — straight away," Jenny replied.

"Okay," I told her. "I'm coming right down."

I peered down at the stage floor. Not that far, I told myself. I'll land easily on all fours.

I raised my front paws. Arched my back. Kicked off with my back paws.

And leapt off the top of the ladder.

I heard screams from down on the stage.

As I plunged down, I saw the clipboard fall from Mr Keanes's hands. I saw Ryan's mouth open in shock. He shot out both hands, as if trying to catch me.

I landed hard on my hands and knees on the stage floor.

Pain roared through my body.

I rolled on to my back.

And let out a startled gasp.

Why did I do that? Why on earth did I leap off the top of the ladder?

Was I losing my mind?

"Help her!" someone shrieked.

The auditorium rang out with shrill, frightened cries.

"Did she fall?"

"Did she jump?"

"Is she okay?"

"Somebody — call for an ambulance!"

I saw Ryan and Freddy and some of the kids in the stage crew running towards me. But I didn't wait for them. I jumped to my feet and ran off the stage.

I bumped past Jenny and bolted up the aisle.

I heard everyone calling to me. But I didn't stop. I didn't want to answer their questions. I didn't want to tell them why I'd jumped like that.

Because I *didn't know* why I'd done it.

I knew I couldn't explain it. I'd been acting so strangely all day. Since breakfast. I hadn't felt right. I hadn't felt like myself.

I knew I had to go somewhere and think about it all. But first I had to find out why Mum was calling me at school.

I burst breathlessly into the head's office. The phone was off the hook on Jenny's desk. I grabbed it up. "Hi, Mum. It's me," I said breathlessly.

"Alison, why are you so out of breath?" Mum demanded.

"I jumped off the top of a ladder!" I blurted out. "It — it was so strange, Mum. I thought I could land on all fours."

I waited for her to reply. But I could hear her saying something to Tanner. A few seconds later, she came back on the phone. "Sorry. I didn't hear you. Tanner always interrupts when

I'm on the phone. What were you saying, Alison?"

"Uh . . . nothing." I no longer felt like explaining it. "What's wrong?" I asked her. "Why are you calling?"

"I need you to come home and babysit Tanner," Mum replied. "Your father and I have to go and see my sister. Some kind of emergency. You know Aunt Emma. She sounded really frantic."

"You want me to come home now?" I asked.

"Please hurry," Mum said. "I don't want to leave Tanner alone. He's in one of his moods."

She sighed. "Poor boy. I think something scared him at school or something. He's been acting so tense."

I didn't really feel like going back into the auditorium. I didn't want to face all the questions from everybody. I was glad to have an excuse to leave.

"I'll be right home," I said.

Mum hurried out as soon as I entered the house. "Make sandwiches or something for dinner," she called to me as she climbed into her car. "I'll try not to be too late."

Tanner was definitely in one of his moods. He sat on the floor in his room, staring at a cartoon show on TV. I tried to chat with him. But he only grunted in reply.

I sat beside him on the floor. He scooted away from me grumpily.

"You just want to watch TV?" I asked.

"Maybe," he replied, not taking his eyes off the screen. Then he turned to me. "Want to watch the rest of that film? *Cry of the Cat?*"

"No way!" I declared. "That video scared you to death — remember?"

He crossed his arms over his little chest. "Then I'm just going to watch cartoons."

"Fine. Let me know when you're ready for dinner," I told him.

"I don't want dinner," he insisted. "You don't know how to make anything good."

What a grump.

At a little after six, he changed his mind. "What's for dinner?" he asked. "I'm starving."

My stomach was growling too. I had a real craving for a big tuna-fish sandwich. But as Tanner and I walked to the kitchen, I remembered that I'd finished all the tuna at breakfast.

"Maybe I'll just have a bowl of milk," I murmured.

"Huh?" Tanner stared at me. "Can I have peanut butter and jam?"

"I suppose so," I replied.

"Very little jam," he insisted.

"I know, I know," I groaned. Tanner has rules for everything. If you put too much jam on the peanut butter, he won't eat the sandwich.

I clicked on the kitchen lights, and we walked over to the food cabinets. I started to ask Tanner if he wanted bread or toast. But something caught in my throat.

I started to cough.

I swallowed hard. And coughed again.

I had an enormous lump in my throat. I couldn't cough it up.

I sucked in a deep breath — and coughed as hard as I could.

My stomach heaved.

The lump caught in my windpipe. I started to choke. I gasped for air.

Tanner's eyes bulged in fright. He grabbed my hand. "Alison, are you okay?"

I couldn't answer him. I was choking. Wheezing. Trying to cough.

Finally, I bent my whole body back — and heaved.

And coughed up the lump. I felt it slide up my throat and roll on to my tongue.

Breathing hard, I reached into my mouth and pulled it out.

"Ohhh." I uttered a groan of disgust.

A wet grey hair ball. As big as a table-tennis ball.

I held the disgusting wad of grey hair in the palm of my hand and stared at it in horror.

"Yuck! That's so *gross*!" Tanner cried.

I turned away from him. I didn't want him to see how frightened I felt.

What is *happening* to me? I wondered.

I knew it had something to do with that cat. Rip.

"Alison, are you ill?" Tanner asked in a tiny voice.

"I — I don't know," I stammered.

I stared down at the disgusting hair ball.

I have to go back to that creepy house, I decided. I have no choice. I have to talk to Crystal. She *has* to tell me what is going on.

I can't wait another day, I told myself. I'll go tonight.

"Alison didn't put enough peanut butter on my sandwich! And she burnt the toast!"

That was Tanner's complaint the second Mum and Dad walked in the door.

"I'm sure she tried her best," Dad said, smiling at me.

"Her best *stinks*!" my kid brother growled.

I stuck out my tongue at him. "Is Aunt Emma okay?" I asked Mum.

She nodded. "Yes. Everything is fine."

"I — I have to go out now," I blurted out.

Dad checked his watch. "It's nearly eight-thirty."

"I promised Ryan I'd help him rehearse his lines for the play." I didn't like lying to my parents. But there was no way I could tell them I had to see a strange girl about a cat I'd killed three times.

A few minutes later, I was jogging down Broad Street, picking up speed as I moved

73

downhill. It was a clear, cool night. A pale half moon floated low over the treetops. The grass on the lawns glistened under a wet dew.

Two big, shaggy dogs came loping along the pavement. They both gazed up at me as I trotted between them. A van filled with teenagers rumbled past, rock music roaring out of its open windows.

I slowed my pace as Crystal's house came into view. I squinted over the weed-cluttered lawn. Pale grey light seeped from the front window.

"She must be home," I murmured to myself.

My trainers crunched over the gravel driveway. I heard the soft cries of cats from inside the house. Several dark figures stared out at me from the window.

I took a deep breath and knocked on the front door. A chill ran down my back despite the warmth of the night.

Inside the house, the cat cries grew louder.

I wiped sweat off my forehead with the back of my hand. Then I nervously pushed my hair back with both hands. And knocked again.

My heart pounded as I waited. Would Crystal know how to help me? Would she be able to explain to me what was happening?

Finally, the front door creaked open. Crystal poked her head out from the cold grey light. She was dressed in a long black pinafore. Even in the dim light, I could see cat hairs all over her dress.

She raised her tired dark eyes to me. "What do you want?" she demanded sharply.

Not very friendly.

"I — I have to talk to you," I stammered. "Do you remember me? I —"

"I really can't talk now," she interrupted. Cats yowled behind her. A scrawny black-and-white cat brushed against her legs.

She started to close the door.

"But I need your help," I insisted. "I need to find out —"

She kept her hand on the door handle. "Is it about Rip?" she asked.

I nodded. "Yes. You see —"

She raised her hand to cut me off. "*Please* — go away!" she cried. Her eyes filled with fear. "Please — I can't!"

I grabbed the door to stop her slamming it shut. "You've got to help me!" I screamed. "You've got to explain what's going on."

"No —" she started. Her chin trembled. Her frightened eyes reflected the eerie grey light. "No. Mum is very unhappy. Mum doesn't want me to talk to you."

"But — just listen to me!" I pleaded. "I killed that cat. I know it sounds crazy. But I killed Rip. I killed him *three times*!"

75

Crystal gasped. She raised her hand to her mouth.

"He — he keeps coming back," I told her. "I killed him, and he came back."

Cats cried from inside the house. Crystal leant closer. The grey light spilled over us. She grabbed my arm. Her hand felt as cold as ice.

"How many times did you kill Rip?" she asked in a whisper.

"Three," I told her. "Three times."

"Noooooooo!" She opened her mouth in a horrified cry. Her cold hand squeezed my arm.

"Why? What's wrong?" I demanded in a trembling voice. "What does that mean?"

"He's used up eight lives," Crystal groaned, shaking her head. "He's used up eight. He'll be desperate now. Be careful. Stay away from him. Rip will be *desperate*."

"I don't understand," I murmured. "Please —"

Her cold hand slid off my arm. I caught one last glimpse of the horror on her face.

Then she slammed the door shut.

"No —!" I cried. "You have to explain! Crystal — please open the door. I have more to tell you. I need your help. He scratched me! Can you hear me? He scratched me!"

The door didn't open. I heard a cat yowl angrily inside. From the doorstep, I could see several cats staring out at me from the grey light in the front window.

"Crystal — listen to me!" I begged. "Rip scratched me. And I've felt so weird ever since."

I pressed my ear against the wooden door. "Are you still there? Can you hear me?"

No reply.

I backed off the doorstep. My legs trembled so hard, I nearly fell. I hugged myself to stop shivering.

"Crystal?" I called. "Crystal?"

The cats stared at me from the window. Their eyes glowed like tiny light bulbs.

I backed on to the drive.

And felt someone grab my shoulders.

With a gasp, I spun round. "Ryan!" I cried. "What are *you* doing here?"

He let go of me and backed up a step. He was breathing hard. "I was riding home in the car, with my parents. I saw you out here," he explained. "I ran all the way back."

He bent over and pressed his hands against the knees of his jeans, catching his breath. "Alison, what's going on?" he demanded. He motioned to Crystal's house. "What are you doing out here? Did you see the cat again?"

I started walking. Ryan hurried to catch up. I turned right at the street, away from my house. I stepped into the deep shadow of a row of tall hedges.

"I had to speak to that girl," I told Ryan. "I had to ask her some questions. But she wouldn't help me."

I crossed the street and kept walking. The houses ended on this block. We passed a small wooded area. The trees shivered in the mild wind.

I'd never walked here before. But for some strange reason, I felt that I knew where I was going.

Across the next street stood a wide, empty plot. Tall weeds tilted and bowed as we moved by.

"Hey — slow down. Why wouldn't she help you?" Ryan asked, jogging beside me.

"Too afraid," I murmured.

"Huh?"

"She was too afraid," I repeated. "Whenever I mention Rip, she starts acting terrified."

"Is he her cat?" Ryan asked.

I shrugged. "She's too scared to tell me anything about it. Crystal is so weird. She keeps talking about her mum. She keeps saying that her mum is unhappy. Her mum won't like what's happening."

"What does her mum have to do with it?" Ryan demanded.

"Beats me." I turned at the next corner. Past a clump of low evergreen shrubs stood another weed-choked plot.

Ryan brushed his dark hair back. "Where are we going?" he asked.

"Huh?" For some reason, his question didn't make sense to me. I struggled to put the words together. But I suddenly felt dazed. As I kept jogging, I glanced round, confused.

"Why are you going this way, Alison?" Ryan repeated breathlessly.

I realized I was running now. In a hurry.

But where was I running? Why had I come this way?

We passed another empty plot. There were no street-lights now. Darkness rolled over us. The wind carried a chill.

I kept running. Ryan trotted close behind.

I'd never been on this street. Why was I here now?

"Alison — stop!" Ryan pleaded. "Where are you leading us? Why are you doing this? Can we stop and talk for a minute?"

I didn't answer him. I turned and cut through the empty plot. Weeds slapped at the legs of my jeans as I ran. My trainers sank into soft, dew-soaked dirt.

Something was pulling me. Something drew me to this spot.

An invisible force had pulled me here.

I felt dazed. Out of control.

I jumped over a low hedge. The half moon slid out from behind a dark cloud. White light washed over us.

The whole world appeared to light up.

Ryan grabbed my hand. "Alison — stop," he whispered. "Look where we are."

I gazed around. Struggled to focus my eyes. Stared at the low stones poking up at angles from the tall grass.

"Alison —" Ryan asked softly, his voice trembling. "Why did you bring us to a cemetery?"

"I — I don't know," I choked out. "Really. I don't know. Something brought me here. Something forced me to come."

Still feeling dazed, I took a few steps towards the low gravestones.

And something reached up and grabbed my ankle.

I opened my mouth in a terrified scream.

Ryan leapt to my side.

He bent down. And pulled off a long root that had tangled around my trainer.

"I thought . . ." My heart pounded. I cleared my throat. "I thought something had *grabbed* me."

Ryan laughed. "Just some kind of root. You walked right into it. I hope you're not getting *too* weird."

I reached down and rubbed my ankle. My head was spinning. My skin felt all prickly.

"Let's get out of here, Alison." Ryan tugged my arm.

"No. Wait." I pulled away from him. And took a few more steps across the wet grass towards the stone grave markers.

The wind blew harder, flattening the grass in front of me. The gravestones glowed dully under the smoky pale light of the half moon.

"The stones — they're all so small," Ryan murmured.

Keeping close together, we stepped into the back row of graves. Stones tilted at different angles. A few had fallen over and lay on their backs, surrounded by tall grass.

I bent down to read the word engraved on a low stone: SPUD.

"What kind of a name is that?" I asked Ryan.

He moved down the row, reading off the names he could make out: SPIKE, MILLIE, FLASH, WHITEY . . .

Ryan turned to me, his features twisted in confusion. "It's a pet graveyard," he announced.

"Huh?" His voice seemed so far away. I squinted through the eerie, pale light at the rows of stones. "Pets?"

"Why did you bring us here?" Ryan asked again. "It's a pet graveyard. All dogs and cats. Look. Here's a dog actually called Rover. I didn't think anyone really called their dog Rover!"

Ryan said something else. He moved down the row of gravestones. His hand trailed along the tops of the stones.

I think he was calling out the names of the dead pets. But I couldn't hear him. I had a low whistling in my ears. Ryan's voice seemed miles away.

The stones rose up in front of me. They

reminded me of rows of jagged, broken teeth.

Ryan's voice faded further into the distance.

I moved through the rows without seeing anything. Without realizing I was even walking.

I felt as if I were floating, floating in a silent world all my own.

I stopped in front of a low stone. The top and sides were cracked and chipped.

I squinted at the name engraved on the front. It was nearly worn off. I had to stoop and bring my face up close to the stone to see it clearly.

The whistling in my ears grew louder. Shriller.

And then it vanished.

I stood in silence.

And stared at the name on the stone: RIP.

My eyes froze on the entire inscription:

RIP. 1981–1993.

"He's dead," I murmured. "He's already dead. That's why I can't kill him. The cat has been dead for years!"

I stared at the gravestone, unable to think, unable to move.

Crystal's words floated through my mind once again: *"He's not an ordinary cat. You shouldn't have messed with Rip."*

Rip is a *dead* cat, I thought.

A dead cat that I killed three more times.

"He'll be desperate now," Crystal had told me. *"That was his eighth life. He'll be desperate now."*

She didn't believe that old tale about cats having nine lives — did she?

I didn't believe it — *did* I?

If he had only one life, he would be dead and buried beneath this stone. Dead and buried in 1993.

He couldn't have run under my bike tyre. He couldn't have climbed over my face and tried to smother me.

If he had only one life, he couldn't have

scratched me. He couldn't have put his bright white mark on me . . .

"Alison — what are you doing?"

Ryan's shrill cry broke into my thoughts.

I felt his hand on my shoulder. But I didn't turn round. And I didn't stand up.

I was down on my knees in the wet grass. The cold dew seeped through my jeans, but I didn't care.

"Alison — what are you doing?"

I knew what I was doing. I was digging up the cat's grave. I frantically scooped up the wet dirt with both hands.

I dug rapidly with both hands, scooping wildly, throwing the dirt behind me. I pawed it up like an animal. My hands burrowed deeper . . . deeper.

I had to see the cat's bones. I had to know he was really down there.

"Alison — let's go!" Ryan stood over me. His voice was high and shrill. "Alison — please!"

I didn't answer him. I didn't want to talk to him. I didn't want to explain.

I didn't want him to see me digging like this, pawing up the dirt so wildly, so desperately.

Deeper . . . deeper. Leaning over the hole.

Those soft animal cries — I realized they were coming from me. "Oh . . . oh . . . oh . . . oh . . ." A low cry with each breath.

Hot sweat dripped down my forehead. My

hands ached. The dirt clung beneath my finger-nails.

"Alison — stop!" Ryan cried. "Alison — you're scaring me. You're really scaring me. Will you stop?"

No, I won't stop.

No, I *can't* stop.

I had to know the truth about Rip. I had to know that he was buried under this gravestone.

I leant in further, pawing, pawing up the dirt.

And then my hands hit something hard.

"Ow!" I cried out, more in surprise than in pain.

Panting like an animal, I began scooping up the dirt harder, faster.

A dark wood box came into view. I wiped the dirt away to uncover the lid. Then one side. Then, scraping the wet dirt away, I saw the whole box.

"The cat's coffin," I heard Ryan murmur behind me. "Alison, what are you going to do with that?"

With a loud groan, I reached down. I grabbed the sides of the dark wood coffin. I tugged it up.

Heavier than I thought.

I slipped. And started to fall head first into the hole.

"No!" I uttered a cry. Caught my balance. Leant in again.

I grasped the sides of the cat's coffin tightly. And pulled it out of the grave.

Panting hard, I slid the coffin on to the dirt. The lid was stained and caked with dirt. I brushed some of it away with my hand.

Ryan stood behind me. "I don't believe this," he muttered. He dropped down on to his knees beside me. "You're really going to open that thing, aren't you."

I didn't answer him.

I was breathing so hard, my throat felt so tight and dry, I didn't know if I could speak.

Shivering, I reached out both hands and grasped the cat's coffin once again. Then I lifted the coffin on to my lap.

I stared at it for a moment. Then I swallowed hard.

I grabbed the lid with both hands — and pulled it open.

Claws raised high, the cat leapt out at me.

I saw the glow of his yellow eyes.

Then I saw the flash of his pointed white teeth.

As he flew out of the coffin, he pulled open his mouth in a shrill hiss of fury.

I didn't have time to move. The open coffin fell from my lap. The cat's paws thudded on to my shoulders, and I toppled on to my back.

I heard Ryan's startled cry over the wild hissing of the cat.

I raised both hands to try to fight the creature off. But his hot, furry body covered my face, and his front paws wrapped tightly round my neck.

He's trying to smother me again, I thought.

I reached up and grabbed his back. We wrestled for a moment, rolling in the wet grass.

I opened my mouth to breathe — and swallowed a mouthful of cat fur.

Choking, sputtering, I struggled to pull the cat off my face.

Above me, I heard Ryan's frantic cries.

And then I felt the cat being lifted away.

I rolled out from under him. Panting hard, I spun to my knees.

Ryan had the cat in both hands, holding him by his middle.

He kicked all four legs furiously, hissing and spitting. His yellow eyes glowed angrily like twin flames.

"Get up, Alison!" Ryan cried, struggling with the thrashing, hissing cat.

I climbed shakily to my feet. My head spun. I tried to blink away my dizziness.

"Run! I — I can't hold on to him!" Ryan groaned.

Rip gave a hard kick. His whole body wriggled and squirmed.

He slipped down. Ryan desperately held on. "Run, Alison!"

Run where?

I took a deep breath and started to move.

"Noo!" I let out a cry as I stumbled over the cat's coffin. I fell over it and dropped hard on my elbows and knees on the grass.

I spun round — and saw the cat slide free from Ryan's grasp. His yellow eyes flared. He bared his curved teeth. Then he lowered his head and came loping towards me.

Ryan stumbled forward. He bent down and grabbed for the cat again.

But the cat whirled and furiously swiped a claw at Ryan's face.

Ryan dropped back.

To my surprise, Rip stopped. And rose up on his hind legs.

Once again, his eyes flashed at me with fury.

And then the cat tilted back his head — and uttered a high, shrill cry. So high and shrill, I had to cover my ears.

Everything seemed to freeze. Ryan. Me. The grey cat on his hind legs, his mouth still opened wide.

We all froze for a second.

And then I heard a low, rumbling sound, and the ground began to tremble.

All around us, the gravestones rocked and bumped against each other. A gravestone thudded over. Two others banged together.

The rumble became a roar.

The grass trembled. The ground rose and fell.

I saw a wisp of black smoke float up from in front of a trembling gravestone.

Another gravestone tilted back, then toppled heavily to the ground.

The graves were trembling and rocking all around us.

Another thin wisp of smoke curled up from a hole in front of a gravestone.

I turned and saw snakes of black smoke shooting up from the graves. Rising up over the grass, then billowing darkly out.

The ground rumbled and shook.

The black smoke rose all around.

The air grew cold, so cold . . .

"What is happening?" I cried in a tiny, terrified voice. "Ryan — what is happening?"

22

Ryan didn't reply.

I searched through the mist for him. But the smoke billowed around me, too thick, too black to see through.

"Ryan?" I called. "Are you okay?"

No answer.

The black smoke swirled around me, circled me.

So cold. The air grew so cold.

A sour smell invaded my nose. An odour like decaying meat.

As the dark mist circled, I began to see shapes. I saw round heads, and thin legs, curling tails — floating together in the billowing mist.

Cats.

Dead cats, I realized.

Ghost cats. Floating up from their graves.

Dozens of ghost cats, swirling darkly around me, their grey eyes glowing dully.

The sour smell swept over me. The air grew colder.

I shivered.

"No — please!" I tried to move. I had to get out of there.

But the cats and the smoke whirled around me like a dark tornado.

The cats eyed me silently, spinning, spinning. In the mist. Part of the mist. Smoke and ghostly cats whirling faster and faster.

I'm trapped, I realized. I can't see — and I can't move.

"Ryan?" I called. "Have they trapped you too?"

No answer.

I started to choke on the smoke. I covered my nose and mouth with one hand. Shielded my eyes with the other.

Can I *run* through them? I wondered.

Are they only smoke? Not solid at all?

Can I run through them and escape?

The sour odour forced its way into my nose. Coughing, I raised my eyes to the dark, swirling cats.

I held my breath. I steadied myself. And then I lowered my head and started to run.

I hit the swirling, smoky tornado with my shoulder.

The blackness washed over me. Swallowed me. Spun over me.

I forced myself forward, my head lowered, my shoulder down.

Ghostly cries echoed around me. Soft cat groans and moans. The groans and cries of dead cats.

Darker . . . darker . . . the mist was alive. Alive with the floating, crying ghosts.

I pushed hard. Lowered my shoulder again. Pressed forward on my trembling legs.

And broke through.

The cool night air rushed against my face. The silvery moonlight shimmered in front of me.

I saw the fallen gravestones. The deep holes dotting the grass, from where the ghosts had escaped their graves.

Where is Ryan? I wondered.

I called out to him. But the cries and moans of the ghost cats behind me drowned out my shouts.

I didn't turn back. I kept running.

I sucked in deep mouthfuls of the fresh air. And I kept moving. My trainers slid on the wet grass. My heart thudded in my chest.

Out of the frightening graveyard now. Across a weed-choked vacant plot of land.

I ran frantically, through the plot, past a row of tall, dark hedges. Crossed a street. Then another.

And heard a steady *THUD* on the pavement behind me.

With a gasp, I glanced back.

And saw Rip trailing me. Eyes on fire. Dark paws trotting over the street. Tail curled up behind him.

He hissed as our eyes met.

I raised my eyes. And behind him, saw the black mist carrying the moaning ghosts.

Following me.

Floating fast. Swirling, spinning as he floated. Sweeping over the street behind me.

Ducking into the wind, I forced myself to run harder. My side ached. My temples throbbed.

The dead cats moaned and cried behind me. So close behind.

Rip's paws thudded the ground.

I turned a corner.

And Crystal's house rose up in front of me. Dark except for the cold grey light in the front window.

Panting like an animal, I forced myself up the front lawn. I lurched on to her front doorstep.

My chest heaving, my whole body aching, I raised both hands and pounded on the front door. Pounded with all the strength I had left.

"Crystal! Help me! Help me!" My voice hoarse with fear.

"Crystal — please! Open the door! You've got to *save* me!"

No reply. Not a sound inside the house.

I turned to the front window. Empty.

"Crystal — please!" I begged. I pounded the front door frantically with both fists. "Crystal?"

I glanced towards the street. Rip had reached the edge of the front garden. He came trotting through the tall grass, eyes glowing brightly, locked on me.

The swirling black cloud, carrying its moaning ghosts, floated close behind him.

"Crystal —" I pleaded. I raised my fists to pound again — and the door swung open.

"Crystal —" I gasped.

She reached out. Grabbed me. And pulled me inside.

She slammed the door hard behind me. And locked it.

"I — I —" I was panting too hard to speak, gasping in mouthfuls of air. I slumped against the wall, waiting for my head to stop throbbing, for the pain in my side to fade.

"It's . . . Rip," I finally choked out. "And cats . . . dead cats . . . they floated up like smoke, and — and . . ."

To my surprise, Crystal threw her arms round me and hugged me. "Oh, Alison, I'm so sorry," she exclaimed. "Really. I'm so, so sorry."

She pressed her cheek against mine and hugged me with real feeling. When she backed away, I saw her pale face twist in worry — and fear.

"I warned you," she whispered. "Rip is not an ordinary cat. Rip won't stop. Not until he gets what he wants."

I swallowed hard. "What does he want?" I choked out.

Crystal lowered her eyes. "Your life," she replied.

"But — why?" I choked out.

Crystal tugged me into the hall. "No time to explain," she insisted. "He picked you out."

"Huh?" I cried. "I don't understand. I —"

A cat cried outside the front door.

I jumped.

"It's Rip," Crystal whispered. "Rip and the other cats. The other cats are his slaves. The locked door won't keep them out."

"But —" I started.

"They'll be in the house in a few seconds,"

Crystal said, her eyes narrowed on the front window. "Come on, Alison. We've got to hurry."

"But can you help me?" I cried, following her towards the back of the house. "Can you protect me from him?"

Crystal pulled me through the back hall. She stopped at a closed door.

I could hear the howls of cats from the front of the house. And I could hear Rip's shrill warning cry.

"Can you help me?" I repeated.

Crystal pulled open the door. I saw only darkness on the other side. "Only Mum can help," Crystal whispered. "Only Mum can save you from him."

I heard heavy thuds in the front of the house. The cat yowls and moans grew louder.

Were the cats inside already?

Crystal clicked a light switch. I saw steep wooden stairs leading down. "Hurry," she urged.

I didn't understand. "Go downstairs?" I asked. "But — where is your mum?"

"Downstairs," Crystal replied. She squinted back at the long hall. "Hurry. Only Mum can help you. Only Mum knows how to take care of Rip."

I gazed down the steep stairway. In the dim grey light, I could see a stone wall down below.

A chill of fear ran down my back. I held back. "Your mum is down there?" I asked.

Crystal nodded. "Don't be afraid, Alison. I'm coming with you. I'll help you."

I took a deep breath. The stairs had no railing. No walls on either side. Nothing to hold on to.

My legs were still trembling from my long, frantic run from the pet graveyard. I shivered again.

"Hurry," Crystal urged.

I took a step. Then another. Slowly, carefully, I made my way down the stairs.

Crystal followed close behind, holding my hand.

When we finally reached the bottom, I let go of her hand and glanced around. Two flickering fluorescent bulbs at the ceiling sent a wash of green-grey light over the long basement.

The room had a long table down the middle, cluttered with tubes, wires, strange scientific equipment. Along the wall, I gazed at a row of machines covered with dials and gauges, wires and cables connecting everything.

"This is Mum's lab," Crystal said softly.

"Is she a scientist?" I asked.

Crystal didn't answer.

Instead, she cupped her hands around her mouth and called out, "Mum? Mum?"

Her voice echoed off the stone walls.

I heard a cough. Then someone stirring from somewhere in a back room. Then I heard slow, scraping footsteps on the concrete floor.

"Mum is the only one who can help you," Crystal repeated, keeping close to me. "Mum has had to deal with Rip . . . and all of Rip's lives."

"Huh? Is Rip really dead?" I whispered. "I saw the grave and . . ." My voice trailed off as the slow footsteps grew louder.

I held my breath and waited. Would Crystal's mum really be able to protect me from that evil cat and all those ghosts?

At the end of the long room, a hunched figure shuffled into view.

"It's Mum," Crystal announced.

I squinted through the grey light at her.

And then I opened my mouth in a horrified scream.

I cut off my scream with my hand. And backed against the stone wall in horror.

Mum had a woman's face — dark lips, a slender nose, dark, oval eyes.

But two pointed cat's ears poked up from her stringy grey hair. And clumps of white cat's whiskers bristled out from both cheeks.

She shuffled closer. She wore a baggy black sweater over a long red skirt.

Her right hand — a human hand — rested on her waist. But dangling from the left shoulder of her sweater was a fur-covered cat's leg with a cat's paw at the end.

A furry cat's tail trailed out from a hole in the back of her skirt. As she made her way to me, I saw fur over the back of her neck.

"Ohhhh." I couldn't hold back a moan of horror.

Half woman, half cat.

Crystal's mum was half human, half creature.

"Sometimes . . . people are surprised by me," she said to me, stepping past Crystal. And then she meowed.

I gasped. "I — I —"

She walked over. Reached down. Grabbed my arm. She lowered her head, and her cat's whiskers brushed my skin.

"Stop it!" I shrieked as her human lips opened and she licked my shoulder with a scratchy tongue.

"Please — stop!"

She stepped back, a hurt expression on her face. "Just cleaning you up a little," she rasped.

She scratched the fur on the back of her neck with her human hand.

A wave of nausea swept over me. She looked so strange, so terrifying.

I realized my whole body was trembling. My legs started to collapse.

I hugged myself tightly. And pressed against the wall to stop myself falling over.

A strange, crooked smile spread over her face. She patted my arm with her cat's paw.

Then her smile faded, and she turned to Crystal. "Is she ready?"

Crystal nodded. "Yes. She is ready."

"You — you're going to help me?" I asked Crystal.

"No," Crystal replied. Her dark eyes locked coldly on mine. "No, Alison. I'm sorry, but we're not going to help you. You are going to help *us*."

"Hold her for Rip," Mum ordered.

25

"No!"

I let out a cry and dived for the stairs.

But Crystal moved quickly to block my path. She wrapped her arms round me and held me in place.

I struggled to squirm free. But she held on tightly. And I felt Mum's cat's arm wrap around my waist.

Mum meowed. Then she brought her face close to mine and whispered, "Don't try to escape. He picked you out. Rip picked you out."

"I don't understand!" I wailed. "Let me go! Let me go!"

Crystal tightened her grip. "You ran over him," she murmured. "You took one of his lives. So he decided you would be next."

"Next?" I cried. "What do you mean?"

Mum's cat's arm tightened around my waist. I couldn't move. I couldn't break free. "You will be next to give up your life for him," Mum declared.

"Huh? Give up my life?" I shrieked. "Did you give up *your* life? *You're* dead too?"

Mum shook her head. Her cat's whiskers brushed my cheek. "No. I'm not dead. But almost. I have no more life to give him. That's why we need you."

She sighed heavily. Then pointed with her human hand to the long lab table. "The experiments all went bad," she said sadly. "My work with the cats — it was all a big mistake."

She shook her head. "All the cats died. I buried them in the pet cemetery. But Rip was too strong to die. Too strong and too evil. He refused to stay dead. And he brought back the other cats to be his slaves."

I stared at her, trembling, unable to believe what I was hearing. "I — I don't understand," I choked out.

Mum pinched my waist with her paw. "Did he scratch you?" she demanded. "Did Rip scratch you?"

I nodded. "Yes. Once. On my leg."

"Every time he scratches you, you become a little more like him," Mum explained. "And every time he scratches you, he takes a little bit of your life. He takes a little bit of *your* life to make sure he doesn't use up all nine of his lives."

"That's how he stays out of the grave," Crystal murmured. "He has used Mum's energy. He has used Mum's life . . ."

Mum sighed again. "You can see with your own eyes what he has done to me. Every scratch made me more like him. He wanted Crystal to give up her life for him. But I wouldn't allow that. I gave up my life to save Crystal's."

Her eyes burned into mine. "But now I have no more life to give," she whispered. "So many scratches . . . so many . . ."

I heard a scraping sound across the room. I turned and saw Rip. He stood on the top stair, his yellow eyes trained on us.

"He's here!" Crystal declared.

"The girl is ready for you!" Mum called to the cat. "The girl has fresh life for you, Rip!"

"Nooooo!" A shrill scream burst from my throat.

"You ran over him," Crystal said, tightening her grip on me. "You owe him, Alison."

"It won't hurt," Mum added. "His scratches are deep. But you never bleed."

"But — but —" I sputtered, my heart pounding in terror. I gaped at Mum. "You mean I'll look like you?"

"It isn't that bad," she replied. "You'll get used to it."

26

I glanced up — and watched Rip move silently down the stairs. He stopped on the bottom step, staring coldly at me, not blinking, not moving his eyes away.

At the top of the stairs, I heard howls and moans. The dead cats appeared, floating above the floor. Their grey eyes glowed dully as they followed Rip down.

Rip moved closer, his tail arched high behind him. His grey fur bristled. He arched his back, preparing to attack.

"She's ready," Crystal told him.

"Alison will take good care of you," Mum told the cat. "Crystal and I are finished here. We are leaving this place for ever. But Alison will stay and keep you alive."

"No!" I uttered with a shriek. And pulled back with all my strength, trying to free myself.

To my surprise, I broke free of Crystal's

grasp. And stumbled back until I hit the wall.

Crystal and Mum cried out. But Rip didn't stop. He trotted steadily towards me, back arched high, fur bristling tensely.

Pressed against the wall, I glanced quickly around. Where can I run? I asked myself. How can I escape?

The dead cats came up behind Rip. Their paws moved as if walking. But they floated thirty centimetres off the floor.

Hissing and crying, they formed a terrifying blockade. I can't get past them, I realized.

There's nowhere to run.

With a loud cry, Rip pulled back on his hind legs.

He's going to leap at me, I saw. He's going to scratch me.

I slid along the wall, edging away.

But I knew it was hopeless. The dead cats formed a solid wall behind him.

Rip raised up higher. His front paws clawed the air.

I prepared to duck.

I'll duck under him, I decided. And then try to break through the wall of ghost cats.

I tensed my body. Waited for the evil cat to leap at me.

I shoved my trembling hands into my jeans pockets. And felt something in one pocket.

What was it? What did I have in there?

My hand squeezed around it. The plastic wind-up mouse. When I'd cleaned up my room, I had shoved it into my jeans pocket.

Rip strutted closer.

I readied myself, prepared to duck.

A noise at the top of the stairs made us all stop and turn.

I heard the heavy thud of footsteps. I gazed up — and saw Ryan.

"There you are!" he called down. "Alison — I've been looking all over for you! What are you doing down there?"

I started to cry out. To warn him.

But Ryan came tearing down the stairs, taking them two at a time.

"No!" I cried, waving him back furiously with both hands. "Ryan — don't come down! Go and get help! Don't come down here!"

He landed hard on the basement floor. Burst through the ghostly wall of cats. Came running across the room towards me. "Alison — are you okay?"

"Ryan — no —" I cried.

Too late.

Rip pulled back his lips and uttered a shrill hiss.

Then he leapt up and furiously scraped his claws down Ryan's arm.

27

"Hunnnnh?"

Ryan opened his mouth in a startled cry of pain.

I stared as the deep white cut spread down his arm.

Rip tilted back his head in pleasure. His eyes closed dreamily.

With an angry shout, I lurched away from the wall. "Ryan — let's *move*!" I cried.

I pulled the plastic mouse from my jeans pocket — and heaved it at Rip.

The mouse hit the cat and bounced to the floor.

As I started to pull Ryan across the room, the dead cats stared at it.

Would they believe it was real? Would it fool them?

Yes!

The cats howled excitedly. And swooped down on the plastic mouse.

Clawing and hissing, they covered it, covered Rip, fighting . . . fighting over it.

I gaped in amazement as they struggled and clawed and bit each other. Rip was lost inside the swirling tidal wave of battling cats.

The other cats swept over Rip, trampled him, smothered him, until he lay lifeless and unmoving. Buried beneath them.

Buried for good?

The dead cats swirled faster and faster, a funnel cloud of biting teeth, flashing eyes, swiping claws.

Faster . . .

Crying . . . all crying now . . . cries so high and shrill, they rose until they became a whistle. A whistle so deafening, I pressed my hands against my ears.

And then — the swirling cloud of battling cats vanished.

Silence.

Still holding my ears, I stared down at the floor.

The plastic mouse lay on its side.

The ghost cats had gone. Rip too. His lives finally used up.

"Ryan — we're okay!" I gasped.

But in all the fury and excitement, I'd forgotten about Mum and Crystal.

And now, side by side, the two of them moved quickly to attack us.

112

Ryan and I froze.

My ears still rang from the shrill whistle of the ghostly cats. I felt dazed and shaky.

Crystal and Mum lumbered across the floor towards us, their expressions hard and cold.

And then smiles broke out on their faces.

Crystal threw her arms around me. "Thank you, Alison!" she cried. "Thank you! You saved us all!"

She pulled me close and hugged me. Mum hugged me too.

The three of us stood in the centre of the room, so happy, so relieved.

Finally, Ryan's voice interrupted our celebration. "I can't believe that stupid plastic mouse got them so excited," he said, shaking his head.

"Cats are still cats," I replied. "Even dead ones."

"Crystal and I are leaving now," Mum

113

said, her human arm around her daughter. "Thank you again, Alison. Thank you a million times."

"Where will you go?" I asked.

"As far away from here as we can," Mum replied solemnly.

"Me too!" I exclaimed. I grabbed Ryan's hand and pulled him to the stairs.

A few seconds later, we were out of that house, into the cool night air. I never looked back.

"Will you sit down for a minute and tell me what's been going on with you?" Mum leant into my bedroom doorway.

"I can't," I declared impatiently. "I'm late for dress rehearsal. You know Mr Keanes goes ballistic if anyone comes late. And this is our last rehearsal!"

It was Saturday afternoon. Our first performance was later that night.

Did I feel a little nervous? You don't need three guesses to answer that one.

"Your father and I haven't seen you for one second," Mum grumbled. "Tanner misses you too."

"I'll spend some time with everybody after the play," I promised. "Now, please. Let me get out of here, Mum. I still don't even know all the songs and —"

"Hey!" Ryan pushed past my mother. "We're late, Alison. What's your problem?"

I sighed and shrugged in reply.

Mum disappeared downstairs. "I'll see you tonight at the play!" she called. "Watch for us. Dad and I will be in the front row. Dad is bringing his camcorder."

"Oh, great," I murmured, rolling my eyes. I turned to Ryan. "I am so stressed out!" I moaned.

"At least we don't have to worry about any more cats," he replied.

"Yes. No more evil cats. Life is back to normal," I agreed. "Now we just have to worry about normal things!"

And then from the next room, a shrill scream of horror made both of us cry out.

Ryan spun to the door.

I was faster. I pushed past him, out into the hall. And burst into my brother's room.

"Tanner!" I cried.

He was on his knees on his bed, chewing the fingernails of one hand.

In front of him, an enormous cat monster was roaring and thrashing its clawed paws.

"Tanner — I thought you'd returned that video!" I cried. "You *know* that *Cry of the Cat* is too scary for you!"

"I — I just wanted to see a few minutes more," he stammered in a tiny voice.

I pushed Stop on the VCR.

The cat monster vanished.

"You scared Ryan and me to death," I scolded. "You can't sit in here and scream like that."

"But I *had* to scream!" Tanner insisted. "It was scary!"

I took the video out of the machine and

116

stuffed it in its box. Then I put it on a high shelf where Tanner couldn't reach it.

I found a cartoon channel for him.

"Are you going to watch the end of the film for me?" Tanner demanded.

"I don't think so," I replied. "Ryan and I aren't cat lovers any more."

A few seconds later, Ryan and I walked out of the back door. I shielded my eyes against the bright sunshine. "Beautiful day," I muttered.

"Beautiful day to be late for play rehearsal," Ryan grumbled.

We made our way along the side of the garage. I took a deep breath, inhaling the sweet aroma of fresh-cut grass. "Dad's just mowed the lawn," I said. "I love that smell."

Ryan didn't seem to hear me. His eyes were on a tall patch of grass the mower had missed at the corner of the garage.

Suddenly, he dived to his knees — and ducked his face into the tall grass.

"Hey — what is your problem?" I cried.

Ryan raised his head and turned to me. He had a big, juicy field mouse trapped in his teeth.

"Hey, give that to me!" I demanded. "I saw it first!"

He shook his head, the mouse dangling from his mouth.

"Give it," I insisted. I swiped at him with a front paw. "Come on, Ryan. Give it to me. I saw it first. Really. I saw it first!"

Welcome to the new millennium of fear

Check out this chilling preview
of what's next from
R. L. Stine

Bride of the
Living Dummy

"Hello, everyone," the ventriloquist began. "I want you to meet my friend Slappy."

Slappy's red-painted mouth slid up and down. "Are we friends?" he asked. He had a shrill, little-boy voice. "Are we really friends, Jimmy?"

"Of course we are," the ventriloquist replied. "You and I are *best* friends, Slappy."

"Then would you do a best friend a favour?" Slappy asked sweetly.

"Of course," Jimmy replied. "What favour?"

"Could you take your hand out of my back?" Slappy growled.

The kids in the audience laughed. I saw Harrison laughing too.

"I'm afraid I can't do that," Jimmy said. "You see, you and I are *very close* friends."

Slappy tilted his head. "Very close friends? How close? Can you give me a kiss?"

"I don't think so," Jimmy replied.

"Why not?" Slappy demanded in a tiny voice.

"I don't want to get splinters!" Jimmy declared.

The kids all laughed. Katie and Amanda thought that was very funny.

Suddenly, Slappy's voice changed. "You don't want to kiss me? Well, I don't want to kiss you, either. Here's a riddle for you, Jimmy," he growled. His voice came out gruff and hoarse. "What's the difference between a skunk and your breath?"

"I — I don't know," Jimmy stammered.

"*I don't know, either!*" Slappy barked.

The kids in the audience laughed. But I saw Jimmy's smile fade. From our third row seats, I could see beads of sweat form on his forehead.

"Slappy — be nice," he scolded. "You promised me you wouldn't do that."

"Here's another riddle for you, Jimmy," the dummy growled.

"No, please. No more riddles," the ventriloquist pleaded. He suddenly looked really upset. I knew it was all an act. But why was Jimmy O'James pretending to be so nervous?

"What do your face and a plate of creamed corn have in common?" Slappy asked.

"I — I don't like this riddle," Jimmy

protested. He forced his smile back. He turned to the audience. "Hey, kids — tell Slappy — "

"What do your face and a plate of creamed corn have in common?" Slappy rasped.

The ventriloquist sighed. "I don't know. What?"

"*They both look like vomit!*" Slappy screamed.

Everyone laughed.

Jimmy O'James laughed too. But I saw more sweat pour down his forehead. "Very funny, Slappy. But — no more insults. Be nice — or I'll have a new job for you."

"New job?" Slappy asked. "What new job?"

"I'll get you a job as a crash test dummy."

"Ha ha. Remind me to laugh," Slappy growled. "You're about as funny as stomach cramps."

"Slappy — please. Give me a break," Jimmy pleaded.

Suddenly, Slappy turned sweet again. "Want to hear a compliment?" he asked. "Can I give you a compliment, Jimmy?"

The ventriloquist nodded. "A compliment? Yes. That's better. Let's hear it."

"YOU STINK!" Slappy shrieked.

Jimmy looked hurt. "That's not a compliment," he said.

"I know. I lied!" Slappy exclaimed. He threw back his head and opened his mouth in a scornful laugh.

Katie and Amanda were on the edge of their seats, leaning over the seats in front of them, laughing. I turned and saw that Harrison was laughing too.

"This man is really funny," Harrison said. "That dummy has a *baaad* attitude!"

"Yeah. I suppose so," I replied.

"You can't even see the ventriloquist's lips move," Harrison said. "He's pretty amazing."

"Jimmy, you should be on the dollar bill," Slappy was saying. "Because your face is all green and wrinkled!"

The twins laughed and slapped the seats in front of them.

"Or maybe you should be on the penny!" Slappy screamed. "Know why? Know why? *Because you're practically worthless!* You're worthless, Jimmy! Worthless!"

Sweat poured down Jimmy O'James forehead. He clenched his teeth and shut his eyes as the dummy screamed at him.

Why does Jimmy look so unhappy, so upset? I wondered.

Why does he look so *afraid*?